UNDEAD PETS

HOUR OF THE DOOMED DOG

For Alice and Archie—SH

For SH and DB, without whom . . .—SC

GROSSET & DUNLAP
Penguin Young Readers Group
An Imprint of Penguin Random House LLC

Text copyright © 2014 by Sam Hay. Illustrations copyright © 2014 by Simon Cooper. All rights reserved. First printed in Great Britain in 2014 by Stripes Publishing. First published in the United States in 2016 by Grosset & Dunlap, an imprint of Penguin Random House LLC, 345 Hudson Street, New York, New York 10014. GROSSET & DUNLAP is a trademark of Penguin Random House LLC. Printed in the USA

Library of Congress Cataloging-in-Publication Data is available.

ISBN 9780448490045   10 9 8 7 6 5 4 3 2

UNDEAD PETS

PETS

HOUR OF THE DOOMED DOG

by Sam Hay

illustrated by Simon Cooper

Grosset & Dunlap
An Imprint of Penguin Random House

The story so far . . .

Ten-year-old Joe Edmunds is desperate for a pet.

But his mom's allergies mean that he's got no chance.

Then his great-uncle Charlie gives him an ancient Egyptian amulet that he claims will grant Joe a single wish . . .

But instead of getting a pet, Joe becomes the Protector of Undead Pets. He is bound by the amulet to solve the problems of zombie pets so they can pass peacefully to the afterlife.

And so the trouble begins . . .

CHAPTER ONE

The hotel's revolving doors whizzed around three times, then Toby burst into the lobby.

"AWESOME!" he squealed. "Your turn!"

Joe grinned at his little brother. He knew they shouldn't be playing in the revolving doors, but it was hard to resist . . .

It was a sunny Friday afternoon and the Edmunds family had just arrived at the Grand Hotel in Skipton Sands. Dad had gone to get the rest of the bags. Mom and Sarah, Joe's big sister, were waiting at the reception desk, and Joe and Toby were supposed to be sitting quietly on the lobby couches.

"Boys!" snapped Mom as the doors spun around again and Joe tumbled out. She gave them that look. The one that meant they were inches away from a mega-blaster scolding!

But Toby was already heading back to the doors.

"Toby!" bellowed Mom. "Stop that at once! You might get stuck."

"Your mother's right," said a voice. It belonged to a silver-haired older lady who had appeared from the office behind the reception desk. "Accidents do happen!"

"Oh, hello," said Mom. "My name's Helen Edmunds. We've got a booking for two nights."

The lady glanced down at a big book on the desk. "Oh yes, you're here for the wedding. Welcome to the Grand Hotel—I'm Mrs. Stanway, the owner. Please call me Sylvia."

UNDEAD PETS

Joe looked around the lobby. It was huge, with a high ceiling and wood-paneled walls. There were lots of weird ornaments everywhere, too—a stuffed fox inside a glass case, a giant vase with a blue whale painted on the side. There was even a collection of samurai swords pinned to a wall.

"Look, Joe!" Toby had found a large brass

gong. He picked up a wooden stick that hung next to it . . .

GONGGGG!

Sarah gave a shriek.

"Toby!" Mom snapped. "Put that down! I'm so sorry," she added to Mrs. Stanway. "He's a bit overexcited about staying in a hotel."

"Oh, don't worry," Mrs. Stanway replied. "The gong isn't valuable. None of my things are. I just like collecting interesting objects." She smiled at Toby. "You should look at the suit of armor on the landing upstairs. My granddaughter says there's a ghost inside."

"Wow!" Toby said breathlessly. "Can I see it?"

"Maybe later," Mom called, but Toby was already racing up the stairs, two at a time.

Joe was about to follow, when he noticed a small dog sleeping near the bottom of the stairs. It had a long thin body and droopy ears, and it was snoring loudly.

"Joe! Give me a hand!" Dad was struggling through the revolving doors, his arms full of luggage. He shuffled forward, then staggered into the reception area, dropping the bags.

The dog looked up and blinked a few times. Joe noticed it had weird eyes—big and staring and green. The dog stood up stiffly, and Joe noticed its short legs. It was a wiener dog! Then suddenly the dog lunged toward Dad . . .

RUFF! RUFF! RUFF! RUFF! RUFF! It was barking at Dad and baring its teeth.

Dad ignored the dog and calmly picked up the stuff he'd dropped.

The dog leaped forward as though it was about to sink its teeth into Dad's ankles.

"Watch out!" cried Joe.

But Dad didn't even look up. "Come on, Joe!" he said impatiently. "Help me with the bags."

"But . . . ," Joe began.

And then the dog stopped barking and sat down. "It's not him. He looked a bit like one of the bad guys for a minute, but he's not!"

Joe gasped. The dog had spoken. This was no ordinary dog—it was an undead pet! That explained why Dad had ignored it—he couldn't see it!

"Hello, Joe," the dog said, turning to face him. "My name is Frankie. I've been waiting for you. There's going to be a robbery, and you've got to stop it!"

CHAPTER TWO

Joe felt a tingle of excitement. An undead pet was the last thing he'd expected to see! They often showed up when Joe was at home, demanding that he solve their problems—they were unable to pass over to the afterlife until he helped them. But he hadn't expected to see one at his cousin Megan's wedding. Maybe the weekend wasn't going to be quite as dull as he'd thought!

"We need to talk!" yelped the dog, who was pacing unsteadily around the lobby.

UNDEAD PETS

Joe noticed it had stitches around its middle, as though it had been chopped in half and stitched back together.

"Are you listening?" the dog snapped impatiently.

Joe nodded, but he couldn't reply in front of his family—undead pets were invisible to them. In fact, they were invisible to everyone apart from Joe. Thanks to the magical Egyptian amulet that his great-uncle Charlie had given him, Joe was the only person who could see the creatures.

"We're on the second floor," said Mom. "Mrs. Stanway says there's a small elevator that we can use to take the luggage up." She handed two bags to Joe—the first was his own duffle bag, the other one was pink.

"Hey!" grumbled Joe, forgetting the undead dog for a moment. "Why do I have to carry Sarah's bag?"

UNDEAD PETS

"Because I'm carrying my bridesmaid's dress!" said Sarah importantly. She pushed past him with a large bag in her arms and followed her parents to the elevator.

Joe rolled his eyes. Sarah being a bridesmaid was all he'd heard about for weeks! She and their cousin Scarlet—another bridesmaid—had been talking on the phone every day about

hairstyles and dresses and shoes.

"There's no room for you, Joe," Sarah called from the elevator. "Take the stairs!"

The elevator doors closed with a *ping*, and Joe was left alone with the undead dog. Even Mrs. Stanway had gone back into her office.

"You'd better tell me what's going on," whispered Joe, sitting down on the bottom step. "Who are you?"

The dog sat up straight with his nose in the air. "My full name is Felix von Frankfurter. And I live here!" He gave an important sniff. "I belong to Sylvia, the lady who owns this hotel. Or at least, I used to . . .

before I died," he added in a smaller voice.

"How did it happen?" Joe

mumbled. "Your death, I mean."

The dog glanced over at the revolving doors. "I had a bit of an accident . . ."

"What? You got stuck in the doors?"

Frankie nodded. "Dachshunds and revolving doors don't really go well together."

Joe looked at Frankie's long, thin body. He could imagine it would be easy for a dog like that to get a bit tangled up.

"Sylvia never let me near them," Frankie sniffed. "I was far too important to her. She always took me out the back way. But last Monday was different. I had to use the revolving doors."

"Why?"

"To chase the bad men!" Frankie growled. His little beady eyes bulged, and the hairs on his coat prickled up like a hedgehog's.

"Calm down," said Joe. "Just tell me what happened."

I was dozing in the hallway when I spotted Sylvia showing two men around . . .

We'll steal it on Saturday. The old woman will never notice!

She said good-bye to them and went back to her office. But the men didn't leave—they stood whispering. I was suspicious, so I crept closer to listen.

I heard them planning to rob the hotel, so I attacked!

Joe grimaced.

Frankie stood up and began to pace around again.

"But why did you bark at my dad?" Joe asked.

Frankie came to a wobbly stop. "Because he looked a bit like one of the robbers. He was wearing the same shorts." Frankie puffed his chest out. "I've been keeping watch in case they come back—like a guard dog!"

Joe smiled. Weren't guard dogs supposed to be big, fierce dogs like Rottweilers and German shepherds?

"And you've got to help, too!" added Frankie.

"Help keep a lookout, you mean?"

Frankie nodded. "AND stop them from stealing anything!"

Just then there was a loud *ding-dong* as a clock chimed in one of the rooms off the hallway.

The hairs on Frankie's coat stood on end. "Time is running out, Joe! You've got to find out what they're going to steal—and quickly, so we can stand guard tomorrow and stop them!"

"Joe?" Dad was coming down the stairs. "Who are you talking to?"

Joe felt his face go red.

"You're not still sulking about having to carry Sarah's bag, are you?"

Joe shook his head.

"Come upstairs and see your room. You've got a great view of the beach."

Frankie gave a whine. "Don't be long, Joe. I'm depending on you!"

"That's mine and Mom's room," said Dad, once they reached the second-floor landing. "Sarah and Scarlet are sharing that one," he added, pointing down the corridor. "And you and Toby are in here."

The room was huge, with two big beds. Toby had already decided which one was his, and was bouncing up and down on it.

"It's amazing!" he said, panting. "We've got our own bathroom! And our own fridge with sodas and chocolate in it!"

"Hey!" said Dad. "You haven't been raiding the minibar, have you? We have to pay for that stuff, Toby. And stop bouncing!"

Joe kicked off his sneakers and stretched out on his bed. It was bigger than his one at

home. And more springy, too!

"Awesome," Joe said. For a moment, he forgot all about Frankie's troubles. "Can we go and explore?"

Just then, Sarah poked her head through the door. "Mom wants to know where her bag with the hair things is. Scarlet and I need to practice our bridesmaids' hairstyles!"

"It's in the dresser in your room, Sarah," said Dad. Then he turned to the boys. "Come on, let's go and check out the beach."

CHAPTER THREE

"Where are you going?" Frankie was waiting for Joe at the bottom of the stairs. He had a sulky look on his face.

Joe glanced around to make sure no one was listening. The lobby was empty, and Toby was already in the revolving doors with Dad close behind.

"I'm going out!" whispered Joe. "To the beach."

"What about the robbery?"

"I won't be long. Anyway, you said it's not

happening until tomorrow."

"What if they come early?" whined Frankie. "They could strike at any time!"

But Joe was already going through the revolving doors. And he was pretty sure Frankie wouldn't follow him in there . . .

"Wow!" Joe murmured, as he walked along the shore with Toby and his dad.

Skipton Sands had a big sandy beach and a long pier with games and rides on it. There were shops selling candy and souvenirs, and there was a tall seawall, where a group of boys were catching crabs.

"Can we do that? Please, Dad!" begged Toby.

"Yeah, can we?" Joe said. "They sell crabbing stuff over there," he added, pointing to a nearby kiosk.

"Go on, then!" Dad pulled out some coins and handed them to Joe.

UNDEAD PETS

A few minutes later he and Toby were back with a large bucket, a net, some fishing line, and a squishy packet of crab bait.

"Ugh!" said Toby when Joe unwrapped it. "Gross!"

"Crabs like it!" Joe squished the bait into the little net bag and then he attached it to the line like he'd seen the other boys do.

He crouched down and dropped the line over the side into the sea.

"Have you got one yet?" asked Toby excitedly, peering over Joe's shoulder.

Just then, Joe felt a slight tug on the line. He quickly pulled it up, but the crab let go of the bait and dropped back into the water.

"Try pulling it up more slowly," Dad said.

Joe tried again, but minutes went by and there was nothing. Then Joe felt a slight tug. This time he pulled gently . . .

"It's massive!" shrieked Toby.

UNDEAD PETS

"Hold it by its back," said Dad as Joe tried to take the wriggling crab off the line. "Then it can't nip you."

"Can we keep it?" Toby asked.

Dad laughed. "I don't think Mom would like a pet crab! No, Toby, they all go back into the sea."

Undead Pets

When Joe had caught three more crabs, it was Toby's turn. Joe was watching the crabs crawling over each other in the bucket, when suddenly something knocked into him . . .

"There you are!" yapped Frankie. "Come quickly! I've seen the robbers on the beach."

Joe glanced over to make sure Dad and Toby weren't watching. "No!" Joe whispered. "I'm crabbing!"

Frankie glared at him. "Come NOW!" he demanded.

Joe scowled and shook his head.

Frankie's eyes bulged, his tail drooped, and he gave a long growl, showing his slimy green gums and sharp yellow teeth. Then he jumped forward and head-butted Joe's bucket, knocking it over.

"Hey!" squealed Joe, trying to grab the crabs

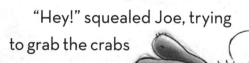

before they escaped. But the biggest one nipped his hand, and all four crabs scuttled back over the ledge into the water.

"No!" groaned Toby.

"Sorry, I knocked them over . . . ," Joe muttered.

Frankie, meanwhile, was busy standing at attention, one ear twitching, and staring off into the distance. And then . . .

"There they are!" he yelped. "The bad guys are on the beach!" Frankie took off like a wobbly rocket, his stitches stretching and bulging as he ran.

"Hello!"

Joe felt a sharp poke in his back and spun around to find Damian, his annoying cousin, smirking at him.

Damian was the same age as Joe, but he was bigger and louder and twice as good at everything. And he made sure Joe knew it!

UNDEAD PETS

"Are you crabbing?" Damian asked, looking down at Joe's empty bucket. "Me too!" He held up a giant bucket full of wriggling crabs. "Where are your crabs?"

Joe frowned. "Well . . ."

Damian snickered. "You should try crabbing over on the other side of the beach. Look how many I've caught!"

"Hi, guys!" Uncle Len, Damian's dad, loomed behind him. He was the size of a grizzly bear— and almost as hairy!

UNDEAD PETS

"Hello, Len," said Dad, shaking his brother-in-law's hand. "When did you get here?"

"Oh, hours ago!" Len said, beaming. "Damian and I wanted to put our new car through the paces."

"It's awesome!" Damian smirked. "A BMW Z4 twin-power turbo!"

"You'll have to come for a spin." Uncle Len grinned. "It's got some amazing gadgets . . . Your dad's not still driving that old clunker, is he?" he added, winking at Joe.

"Where's Kate?" asked Dad, changing the subject.

Aunt Kate, Damian's mom, was Joe's mom's older sister.

"Back at the hotel, talking weddings." Len pretended to yawn. "We thought we'd escape to the beach. It looks like you had the same idea!"

"Look!" shouted Toby. "I caught it!" He held

up the tiniest crab Joe had ever seen.

"Nice job!" Uncle Len smiled. "Shall I take a photo of you boys with your crabs?" Then he looked down at Joe's empty bucket. "Where are yours, Joe?"

CHAPTER FOUR

"Wow!" shrieked Toby, as they walked through the archway onto the pier. "If you hook a duck, you win a fish."

"No way!" muttered Joe. He'd recently had a run-in with a very grumpy undead goldfish, and it had put him off fish for life!

"Over here!" called Damian, who was standing by another stall with Dad and Uncle Len. "Bet I can knock a coconut off before you, Joe!"

The boys paid their money and picked up

their weapons—three little yellow beanbags each!

DONK!

"YES!" shouted Damian, as his first beanbag knocked down a coconut.

DONK!

Another one fell.

DONK!

Damian took down the third coconut and punched the air triumphantly.

"Your turn, Joe!" said Damian smugly.

SPLAT!

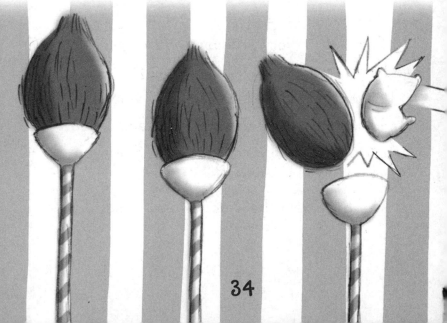

UNDEAD PETS

Damian snickered as Joe's bag hit the back of the tent. "Come on, Joe! It's easy!"

Joe tried again.

THUNK!

His beanbag fell short, landing on the floor.

"Tough luck, Joe," called Dad.

"Don't try so hard," boomed Uncle Len. "Do it like Damian!"

Joe resisted the urge to throw his last beanbag at his cousin's head. Instead, he hurled it at a coconut.

"YES!" yelled Toby, as the bag hit the coconut. It wobbled . . . but stayed in its cup.

Joe let out a groan.

"You need more practice." Uncle Len laughed and high-fived Damian.

"That's one–nothing, me!" Damian said to Joe.

"What?"

"I beat you! So that's one game for me, and none for you."

Joe scowled. It was always the same with Damian. Everything was a competition.

"Joe's great at the claw machine," said Toby.

"The what?" Damian's eyes narrowed.

"You know . . . the grabber thing that picks up a prize?" explained Toby.

"Show me," said Damian.

They raced into the arcade, straight toward a big glass box stuffed with toys and candy.

"Easy," said Damian, putting his money in

the slot. "I'm going for the skull!" He wiggled the joystick, and the claw began moving until it was almost directly above a small plastic skull filled with candy.

"Just a bit more . . . ," said Damian.

But then the machine began to flash.

"It's about to grab!" squealed Toby.

"I'm not ready," wailed Damian as the claw dived down to grab the skull.

"Missed." Toby beamed triumphantly.

The empty claw returned to its position.

"That's not fair." Damian glared. "No one told me I was up against a timer!"

"It gives you thirty seconds to get in position," explained Joe. "Then it grabs."

Joe put his coin into the slot.

"Go, Joe!" cried Toby.

Carefully he edged the claw until it was right above the skull . . .

But then Frankie thundered into the arcade

and charged at him.

Joe jerked the lever wildly. "NO!" he shouted.

"Ha!" Damian snickered. "You missed, too!"

"JOE! JOE!" barked Frankie, pawing at Joe's ankle with his claws. "I lost the men on the beach. You've got to help me find them!"

"I nearly had it," groaned Joe.

"Yeah, yeah." Damian smirked. "Look—air hockey! Come on, Toby, I'll take you on. Maybe you're better than your brother!"

When they'd gone, Joe turned on Frankie. "I almost had that prize."

"You're supposed to be helping ME," growled Frankie, his green zombie eyes flashing.

Joe crouched down and pretended to fiddle with his shoelaces in case anyone was watching. "Listen, what are you going to do if you find the robbers, anyway?"

Frankie cocked his head to one side as though he was thinking about it. "Spy on them."

"How will that help?"

"They might say what time they're coming on Saturday."

Joe rolled his eyes. "That's crazy! Bad guys don't lie around the beach shouting about their next crime."

Frankie glared at Joe. "What are we going to do, then?"

Joe paused. He hadn't really thought about

it. "We'll have to go back to the hotel and keep watch," he said finally. "And try to find out what they're going to steal."

Frankie jumped to his feet. "Great plan. Let's go!"

"Soon," whispered Joe. He could see Damian waving to him from the air-hockey table. "First I've got to beat my cousin!"

Half an hour later, Joe had lost every game that Damian had challenged him to. They finally left the arcade and walked back onto the pier.

"Can we get some ice cream?" Toby asked, peering in a café window.

Dad shook his head. "Mom just texted. She's wondering where we are."

"Please, Dad," Toby whined.

"I bet I can eat more ice cream than you!" hissed Damian in Joe's ear.

UNDEAD PETS

"I'd love a sundae," Uncle Len exclaimed. "Come on. My treat!"

"I think we should head back . . . ," began Dad.

But Uncle Len was already pushing open the café door. "Grab that table by the window, Damian. I'll get more chairs."

The five of them crowded around the only empty table in the café, and Uncle Len waved to a waitress to take their order.

"What's everyone having?" he asked.

"Death by Chocolate!" said Damian. "With extra whipped cream and sprinkles."

"Me too!" Toby's eyes were wide like saucers.

"No, Toby," said Dad. "You'd never finish a big sundae. Choose something smaller . . ."

"What are you having, Joe?" Damian smirked.

"A large banana split, please," said Joe. "With extra chocolate sauce."

"Do you want nuts on top?" asked the waitress.

"Yes, please, and sprinkles, too!"

Dad frowned. "Can you eat all that, Joe?"

"Of course he can!" Uncle Len grinned. "And I'm paying—so everyone can have what they like."

"I bet I finish first!" hissed Damian.

"What about me?" Frankie whined from under Joe's chair. "Sylvia always lets me lick her ice cream."

Joe glanced down at Frankie. The undead dog's mouth was watering and a little pool of green zombie drool was collecting on the floor.

Joe shuddered. He definitely didn't want to share his sundae with Frankie!

The dog began to moan pitifully.

The waitress appeared with their sundaes. Joe gulped when he saw the size of them—his banana split was as big as a beach ball!

Frankie head-butted Joe's ankles. "Where's mine?"

UNDEAD PETS

Joe ignored Frankie and began digging in. But with every spoonful, Frankie's moans became louder and louder . . .

"What's the matter, Joe?" Damian was waggling his spoon at him. "Is the ice cream too much for you?"

Frankie began to howl, and then he grabbed the edge of the plastic tablecloth with his teeth and tugged!

Joe looked in horror as his banana split splattered across the floor.

CHAPTER FIVE

"You should have seen it." Damian smiled. "There was ice cream everywhere. Everyone was staring!"

Joe scowled at his cousin. They were back in the hotel now, sitting in the hotel lounge with Mom and Aunt Kate. Uncle Len and Dad had gone off to play pool. Sarah and Scarlet were sitting a few tables away with the bride-to-be, Megan, and some of her friends. Frankie was in the lobby, keeping watch. Joe was glad. He still wasn't speaking to the crazy dog after the ice-cream incident!

"Don't worry about your sundae," said Aunt Kate. "You should have seen the mess Damian got into on summer vacation last year . . ."

The smile vanished from Damian's face.

"He knocked a whole plate of spaghetti onto his lap!" Aunt Kate beamed.

"No, I didn't!" snapped Damian.

"He was so embarrassed," Aunt Kate said with a giggle. "Especially since there was a bunch of teenagers at the next table," she went on. "They thought it was hilarious!"

"No, they didn't!"

"He ruined his favorite jeans, too," added Aunt Kate.

Damian glared at his mom.

"Oh, look!" Mom exclaimed. "There's Great-Aunt Marion and Great-Uncle Bob!" She waved to an old couple who'd appeared in the lounge.

UNDEAD PETS

"Helen! Kate!" The older woman swept over, gathering Joe's mom and her sister up in a huge hug. Then she turned to the boys. "And this can't be Joe and Toby? And Damian, too! Wow, look how you've all grown! What handsome boys!" Joe grimaced as she hugged him. Great-Aunt Marion smelled of stinky perfume and she left a big lipstick kiss on his cheek!

UNDEAD PETS

Over the next few hours, the lounge gradually filled up with relatives and family friends arriving for the wedding the next day. Joe lost count of the number of people who hugged and kissed him and told him how big he was.

It was nearly nine o'clock when Mom came over to where Joe and Toby were playing cards with Great-Uncle Bob. "I hadn't realized it was so late," Mom said. "It's time for bed."

"I'm not tired!" wailed Toby.

"I never go to bed at the same time as Toby!" added Joe.

Damian looked up from his portable games console and smirked. No one was sending *him* to bed!

"Can't I stay up a bit longer?" pleaded Joe.

"It's just for tonight, Joe. I need you to keep an eye on Toby for me."

"But, Mom!"

"How about a game of mini golf in the morning?" said Dad, trying to cheer Joe up. "Mrs. Stanway was telling me there's a course near the beach."

"Great idea!" boomed Uncle Len. "Count me and Damian in."

"Good plan," said Mom. "It'll give me a chance to start on the girls' hair!"

Joe's mom was a hairdresser, and Megan had asked her to help out with the bridesmaids'

UNDEAD PETS

hairstyles for the wedding.

"I bet you five bucks I win at mini golf!" Joe whispered to Damian.

Damian's eyes glittered. "You're on!"

As Joe followed his mom and Toby out of the lounge into the hall, Frankie appeared. He was wagging his tail innocently, as though the ice-cream drama had never happened.

As Joe and Frankie walked through the hall, the clock in the dining room chimed.

"Nine o'clock, and no sign of the robbers!" Frankie reported, as though he was a soldier on guard.

"Great," murmured Joe.

UNDEAD PETS

"Have you figured out what they're after yet?" Frankie asked.

Joe hung back as Toby and Mom headed for the stairs. Toby was telling Mom all about the haunted suit of armor.

"Dunno!" Joe shrugged. "Money? Jewels?"

Frankie gave a disgusted snort. "How can we stop them if we don't know what they're going to steal?"

Before Joe could answer, he heard footsteps. Mrs. Stanway walked out of the lounge carrying two cash boxes, balanced one on top of the other. Frankie's tail began to drum on the floor and he let out a little whimper of delight at the sight of his owner.

"Hello, young man," she called, smiling at Joe. "Are you having a nice time?" As she spoke, she stumbled slightly on a crease in the carpet and dropped one of the boxes.

Joe rushed over to help. Then he gasped.

UNDEAD PETS

The box had opened and spilled money out . . .

"Thank you, darling," said Mrs. Stanway as Joe pushed the bills and coins back in the box. "I've been emptying the registers in the bar."

"Can I help you carry it?" Joe asked.

"That's very nice of you," Mrs. Stanway replied with a smile.

Frankie trotted after them.

UNDEAD PETS

Inside the office, under a large, messy desk, was an old metal safe.

"My grandfather brought it back from Chicago," explained Mrs. Stanway proudly. "They don't make them like this anymore!"

She twirled a small dial on the front, first one way and then the other. The door creaked open. Joe's eyes nearly popped out. The safe was stuffed with money!

UNDEAD PETS

"All ready for the bank on Monday," explained Mrs. Stanway, emptying the boxes and shoving the cash inside. She tried to close the door, but it wouldn't shut properly. "Oh no! The door's a bit of a pain!" She gave it another shove, and this time it closed.

As Joe and Frankie went back into the lobby, a thought was forming in Joe's brain.

"I bet that's what the thieves are after," he murmured. "The cash in the safe!"

Frankie growled. "OUTRAGEOUS! How dare they!"

"There must be thousands in there," added Joe. "And it wouldn't take much to get the door open!"

"So, what's the plan?" demanded Frankie. "How can we stop them from stealing Sylvia's money?"

"We'll have to keep watch outside the office tomorrow."

"All day and all night!" growled Frankie. "The thieves could strike anytime!"

Joe was just about to explain that he couldn't keep watch ALL day—he had the wedding to attend—when a voice called down from the landing above . . .

"There you are, Joe!" It was Mom, and she looked upset. "One minute you were behind us, the next you'd disappeared!"

"Oh, I'm sorry, I'm afraid that's my fault," said Mrs. Stanway, coming out of her office. "Joe was helping me carry the cash from the bar. I hope that was all right?"

"Oh, of course," said Mom. "That was very nice of you, Joe."

"Good night, darling," Mrs. Stanway said. "See you in the morning."

CHAPTER SIX

Frankie came for Joe at first light.

Joe was dreaming about Damian being swallowed up by a giant squid when the zombie dog dived on top of him.

"GET UP, JOE!"

"What? *Ahhh!* YUCK!" Joe tried to wriggle away as a big dollop of drool dribbled out of Frankie's mouth and onto his face.

"Get up!" Frankie barked again, his scratchy tongue licking Joe's hair. "It's Saturday. The robbers could come anytime!"

Undead Pets

"Go away," Joe hissed. "It's too early!" He glanced over at Toby, who was still sleeping peacefully. Thank goodness he was a heavy sleeper!

"GET UP!" Frankie grabbed Joe's sheet in his teeth and hauled it off the bed. "I need you!"

"Hey!" Joe wrestled the covers out of Frankie's mouth, and pulled them back over his head. "Later!"

Frankie poked his nose under the edge of the sheets. Then he scrambled up and under the covers, grabbed Joe's pajama shorts with his teeth, and tried to yank him out of bed.

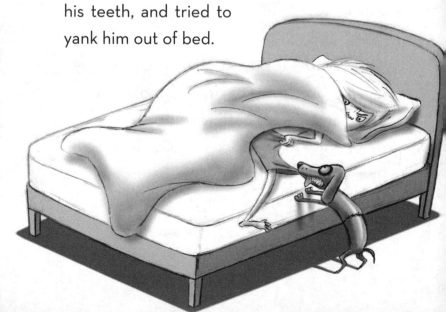

UNDEAD PETS

"Get off!" Joe held on to his shorts. But so did Frankie. Joe pulled and pulled and then . . .

PING!

Frankie let go, and the elastic snapped back. The dog fell out of the bed and everything went quiet.

Suspiciously quiet.

Joe peeped out from under the covers. Frankie was sitting in the corner of the room chewing something.

Joe shot out of bed. "My new sneakers!"

He grabbed one out of Frankie's mouth.

"Ugh!" The laces were slimy and dripping with zombie drool.

Frankie growled. "Come and help me or I'll pee in the other one!"

Joe sighed. "Okay, I'm coming!" He rubbed the sleep out of his eyes, pulled on his jeans, and headed for the door. He glanced back. Toby was still fast asleep and snoring.

DING-DONG! DING-DONG!

The clock in the dining room was chiming six o'clock.

Joe put his fingers in his ears. "Does that clock ever stop chiming?"

"That's Sylvia's favorite clock!" said Frankie huffily. "It's very special. It belonged to her great-grandmother!"

Joe rolled his eyes.

"I always knew when it was time to eat," added Frankie, "or to go for a walk, or to go to bed! I love that clock!"

"Okay, okay! I get it." Joe yawned.

They were in the lobby crouching behind a giant potted palm tree, keeping watch over Mrs. Stanway's office. So far the only person they'd seen was the mailman pulling up outside the hotel and dropping off a package.

UNDEAD PETS

Joe stretched out his legs. They were stiff from sitting for so long. Then his tummy rumbled. "I wonder when it's breakfast time," he whispered.

"Listen," Frankie yelped. "Someone's coming!"

The revolving doors were moving . . . Joe gulped.

"There he is!" yelped Frankie as a tall figure emerged. Frankie leaped forward, barking and growling.

Joe sprang out of their hiding place. He wasn't sure what to do—block the robber's way or shout for help? But then he looked at the thief . . .

"Uncle Len?"

"Morning, Joe, you're up early!" Uncle Len was wearing a bright red tracksuit, and his face was hot and sweaty. "I've just been out for a morning run. Did I tell you I'm training for a marathon?"

Frankie's tail drooped. "Oops."

"Do you want another piece of toast, Joe?" asked Dad.

It was a couple of hours later, and everyone was in the dining room eating breakfast. Joe's family was sitting with Damian and his mom and dad. Frankie was still in the lobby keeping watch.

DING-DONG! The noisy clock on the dining-room mantelpiece chimed.

Uncle Len glanced up from his paper. "Nice clock!" he murmured. Then he turned to Dad.

UNDEAD PETS

"Did I tell you I collect antiques?"

Dad smiled politely.

"I've been collecting for years. You'd be surprised at what you can pick up at flea markets." He tapped his nose. "You just need to know what you're looking for. Take that clock over there; it's an amazing piece—"

"Mom, can you redo my nails before the wedding?" interrupted Sarah, peering at her hands. "One of them is chipped!"

"I'll do them," said Aunt Kate. "Your mom's going to be too busy."

Mom nodded. "When Great-Aunt Marion heard I was doing Gran's hair, she asked me to do hers, too! And then Aunt Sheila asked. And Cath. Even Uncle Bob wondered if I could fit him in for a trim!"

"I wish you could do something with Len's hair!" Aunt Kate grinned. "He looks like a yeti!"

Toby giggled.

Uncle Len looked up, annoyed. "What's wrong with my hair?"

Just then, a waitress appeared and put down another pitcher of orange juice on the table.

"You'll be busy today," Mom said to the waitress, trying to divert Len and Kate from an argument, "with the wedding and everything . . ."

"Oh, it won't be too bad," said the waitress. "Mrs. Stanway hires lots of extra staff to cover weddings, so there'll be plenty of help." She smiled and moved on to the next table.

"Is Uncle Charlie coming to the wedding?" asked Aunt Kate.

Joe looked up. It was Uncle Charlie who had given him the magical Egyptian amulet that had brought all the undead pets to his door.

"Megan invited him," said Mom. "But she didn't get a reply. He's probably up on a mountain somewhere. I haven't heard from him for months."

Joe hadn't either. When the zombie creatures had first begun to arrive, Joe had tried to get in touch with his uncle to tell him what was happening. But he'd only received one postcard. That wasn't unusual. Uncle Charlie was an explorer, and he was usually out of contact for months at a time.

Damian burped and pushed his plate away. "Ready to lose at mini golf?"

CHAPTER SEVEN

As they left the hotel to play mini golf, Joe spotted Frankie asleep in the hallway. He tiptoed past. Hopefully he'd be back before Frankie realized he'd gone!

The Jolly Roger Adventure Golf course was only a few minutes' walk from the hotel. There was a huge plastic pirate outside, and all the obstacles were pirate-themed—wooden barrels, treasure chests, cannons, and sea monsters.

"Good shot!" called Uncle Len, as Damian's

ball whizzed up a ramp and into a skull's eye socket, before dropping out the other side and landing with a *thud* on the grass below. Joe had matched Damian shot for shot on the first five holes. But the sixth one looked trickier . . .

"Give it a good whack!" boomed Uncle Len, as Toby lined up to take his turn. "You'll need plenty of power to get up that ramp."

Toby blasted the ball, but it zoomed left, missing the ramp completely and landing in the bushes.

"Maybe you should take it again." Dad smiled as Toby went searching for it.

"No way!" Damian snapped. "Every shot counts. Your turn, Joe."

Joe lined up his ball . . .

WHACK!

It shot up the ramp, straight as an arrow, into the skull's eye . . .

Joe listened for the THUD as it came out

the other side and hit the grass. But there wasn't one.

"It didn't come out!" called Toby.

Joe bent down and peered inside the skull's mouth.

A small hairy face with bulging green eyes peered back.

"There you are, Joe!" yelped Frankie. "You sneaked off without telling me!"

"Did you swallow my ball?" Joe whispered.

Frankie burped. "Maybe!"

Joe tried to grab him, but the little dog slipped away and jumped out the back of the obstacle.

"Can you see it, Joe?" called Dad.

"No. It must have gotten stuck in the skull somewhere . . ."

"Ha!" Damian giggled. "I win this hole!"

"Go and get another ball from the cabin," said Dad. "You can catch up to us."

Joe trudged off, and moments later he heard the scuttle of small paws.

"Stop, Joe! You've got to listen to me. The robbers are in the hotel! NOW!"

"Go away!"

"They really are, Joe. It's them! I saw them! They're in the lobby of the hotel. We've got to stop them from stealing Sylvia's money!"

"Get lost!"

Frankie bared his teeth and let out a growl. "How dare you! You're supposed to be helping me!"

Joe glared back. "Why should I? You've just ruined the game! For once I had the chance to beat Damian, then you ate my ball!"

Frankie stopped looking fierce, and

a puzzled expression appeared on his face. "Was the game really that important?"

"What? Me beating Damian?" said Joe. "Yes! He beats me at everything!"

Frankie thought for a moment, then suddenly he coughed a few times and spewed up Joe's ball.

"Ugh! Gross!" Joe said, as the ball dropped to the ground, dripping with goo.

"Quick! Go and finish your game," said Frankie. "But just for five minutes! Sylvia was working in her office when I left, so the robbers won't be able to steal anything from the safe yet." Then Frankie turned and raced back to the others.

Joe picked up his slimy ball and caught up to the others at the seventh hole.

"Only three more to go," crowed Damian. "And you lost the last one, Joe. Looks like you'll be paying me five bucks!"

UNDEAD PETS

"We'll see about that!" growled Frankie. "Listen, Joe, there's a bump under the green on this hole. It makes your ball go left, so aim right!"

Joe frowned. How did Frankie know that?

"I've been here lots of times," declared the dog airily, "with Sylvia and her granddaughter. Now remember, hit your ball to the right!"

The hole was supposed to be a crocodile swamp. You had to hit your ball straight down

the middle, past several crocodiles, and into a giant crocodile's mouth.

"This is gonna be easy!" boasted Damian, as he lined up to take his first shot.

WHACK!

It was a good shot—straight through the small gap between the crocodile heads. But just as Frankie had predicted, the ball went wildly off to the left.

"What?" Damian's eyes nearly popped out.

"There must be a bump in the green," suggested Uncle Len. "Aim to the right, Damian!"

Damian took his shot again. He deliberately aimed the ball to the right this time.

But Frankie was restless now. He was pacing up and down the course, and he didn't see Damian's ball coming toward him . . .

THWACK!

It bounced off Frankie's side and landed in the rough again.

Frankie jumped and let out an angry bark. "OUTRAGEOUS!"

Damian grabbed his ball and gave it a final angry hit.

This time the ball sailed over the hole and landed with a splash in a little pond.

"I think it might be your turn, Joe," said Dad, trying not to laugh.

The game was over pretty quickly after that.

Damian was so upset that he totally missed the target on the next two holes as well.

"Come on, Joe!" said Frankie, racing ahead. "We've got to stop the robbery!"

"I'm coming," Joe whispered. He'd beaten Damian. Now it was time to beat the bad guys!

When they got back to the hotel, there were people everywhere. The wedding was due to take place in the hotel gardens in less than an hour, and the guests were milling around.

Frankie stared up at the sea of faces. "Where are the robbers?" he yelped. "I saw them arrive! Where are they now?"

"There you are!" said Aunt Kate. "Damian! Go and get changed at once. And Joe—you and Toby, too . . ."

"You can't go," wailed Frankie. "You've got to help me find the robbers!" He was weaving in and out of the crowd, staring up at all the wedding guests.

"What do they look like?" whispered Joe.

"Tall and thin. One has black hair. One has brown hair."

Joe sighed. That could describe most of the men in the hotel.

"Come on, Joe!" Dad said, guiding him toward the stairs. "We've got to get dressed now."

"Don't go!" barked Frankie. Then he was swallowed up in the crowd of guests.

Joe tugged at his collar. He was thinking about the robbery. This would be the perfect time for the thieves to strike, when there was so much happening in the hotel. It would be easy for someone to sneak into Mrs. Stanway's office. "Can I go down now?" he asked Dad.

UNDEAD PETS

"Go ahead, Joe," Dad replied. "We'll be along in a minute."

Joe raced out of the room.

"Watch it, squirt!" snapped Sarah as Joe nearly collided with her and Scarlet on the stairs. They were wearing their lilac bridesmaids' dresses and walking incredibly slowly!

Joe dodged past them and charged down the last few steps. He had to find Frankie . . .

"Yoo-hoo!" Gran was waving to him from the middle of the lobby.

Joe hesitated, then stopped to say hello.

"You look very smart, Joe," she said, linking her arm through his. "Shall we go out to the garden together?"

"Um." Joe looked around for Frankie but couldn't see him anywhere.

Just then the clock in the dining room began to chime . . .

"Ladies and gentlemen," called Mrs. Stanway. "If you'd like to make your way outside and take your seats, the wedding will begin shortly."

Gran squeezed Joe's arm. "Exciting, isn't it!" As they followed the guests outside, Joe glanced back toward Mrs. Stanway's office. Would the thieves strike now, while everyone was in the garden?

CHAPTER EIGHT

"We are here together to share Megan and Scott's special day," said the officiant who was conducting the service.

Joe couldn't concentrate on the wedding. He kept looking around the garden, wondering where Frankie was and what was happening with the thieves. He couldn't exactly sneak off to see. He was in the middle of a row of guests with Gran on one side and Dad on the other.

"That'll be you one day, Joe!" giggled Gran.

When the ceremony was all over, Joe finally

thought he could go and find Frankie. But just as he was about to escape, the photographer started to speak.

"Can I have the bride's family over here, please?" he called.

"That's us!" said Mom, grabbing Toby's arm. "Come on, Joe, you too."

They were herded together into a corner of the garden where Megan and Scott had been having their pictures taken with Scarlet and Sarah and the best man.

"Smile, Joe!" Mom as she straightened his tie. "You look miserable!"

"That's wonderful," said the photographer as they lined up on either side of Megan and Scott. "If the children could just move a little bit farther forward, so I can see them . . . And bridesmaids, hold your flowers up a little bit higher . . . Perfect. Smile, everyone!"

And that's when Frankie arrived. He came

hurtling across the grass, barking and yelping, "JOE! JOE!"

Joe turned and looked.

Click! Click! Click!

"Great," said the photographer. "Oh no! Wait a minute," he said, peering at his screen. "That boy there . . ." He pointed at Joe. "He wasn't looking at the camera."

Everyone stared at Joe.

"Loser!" hissed Damian.

"I'm afraid we'll need to take it again," said

the photographer. "That's it—back in position. Smile, everyone!"

But now Frankie had reached Joe and was head-butting his ankles wildly. "They're over there!" he yelped. "The robbers! Look!"

Joe looked.

Click! Click! Click!

"Young man!" said the photographer. "Will you please look at the camera?"

"Joe!" Sarah glared at him.

"Concentrate!" whispered Mom.

This time Joe stared at the camera—his face fixed in a mad grin while Frankie barked and yelped, demanding his attention.

"You looked like a total idiot!" muttered Sarah, as everyone moved away.

"There they are!" barked Frankie. "Look!"

Joe looked. But all he could see were a few waiters handing out drinks and snacks.

"Where?"

"The waiters, Joe. It's them!"

Two tall, thin men. One with black hair. One with brown.

"Are you sure?" Joe whispered.

"Definitely!"

It was the perfect disguise for thieves. Dressed as waiters, they could go anywhere in the hotel and no one would notice.

"They must have been here for their interviews on the day I died," said Frankie. "I remember Sylvia talking about needing extra staff for the wedding."

"Sneaky!" murmured Joe.

"We've got to stake out the office!" said Frankie. "Come on, Joe."

For the next hour, Joe and Frankie lurked behind the potted plant in the lobby, watching Mrs. Stanway's office. But no one came near it.

A couple of times they caught sight of the waiters carrying things into the dining room for the wedding meal, but they didn't look interested in Mrs. Stanway's office.

"When are the robbers going to make their move?" whined Frankie, as the waiters carried more trays of glasses into the dining room.

Joe shrugged.

Just then, Dad appeared.

"Joe?"

"Hi, Dad." Joe peered around the side of the plant.

"Why are you hiding out here?"

"Um . . ."

"Look, I know you're not that interested in talking to your relatives, but you can't avoid them all day. Come and have a drink—we're just about to go in for dinner."

"No!" wailed Frankie.

But Dad was already steering Joe back toward the lounge. "You can keep Damian company—he looks really fed up!"

"Great!" muttered Joe.

"More for me, please!" said Uncle Len, holding his glass up for a waitress to refill.

They were halfway through dinner, and Joe was supposed to be keeping a lookout in case the two waiters tried to sneak off while everyone was eating. Meanwhile, Frankie was guarding the lobby. But there wasn't any time for the waiters to sneak off. They were busy.

UNDEAD PETS

Joe glanced around their table. As usual, he and Damian had been put next to each other.

"Can I have a turn?" Joe asked Damian, who was playing on his games console.

"No!"

Joe sighed. He tried listening to the grown-ups talking instead. Uncle Len was dominating the conversation.

"Of course, I've always loved collecting antiques. Take that clock on the mantelpiece right over there—it's very rare, incredibly valuable . . ."

Joe tuned out. Then he looked up and noticed that the two waiters had disappeared. He felt his heart beat faster. Somehow he had to get away and see what they were up to.

CHAPTER NINE

"I'm just going to the bathroom," Joe muttered, getting up from the table.

He dashed back into the hallway and found Frankie barking wildly.

"One of the robbers is in Sylvia's office!"

"What? Now? Why didn't you come and find me?"

"I was just about to! You've got to stop him! Quick, Joe!"

"I'll get Dad . . ."

"No!" wailed Frankie. "He might escape!"

Joe looked at the door. He had to find a way to trap the thief inside! He searched around for something to block the doorway.

"Maybe we could move that big vase," Joe began. But then he spotted something even better. "Look, Frankie! There's a key in the lock!"

Joe dashed around the back of the reception desk and turned the key in the lock.

"We've done it!" Joe beamed. "We've caught the thief!"

The door handle rattled, and there was an angry shout. The man began to bang on the door and yell, "LET ME OUT!"

"What's going on?" Mrs. Stanway appeared next to them. "Who's in my office?"

Frankie gave a whimper of joy. "Tell her what we've done, Joe. How we've saved her cash!"

"Where's Dale?" Mrs. Stanway asked.

"Dale?" Joe frowned.

"Yes, he's a waiter. I sent him to grab my spare pair of glasses from the office. I seem to have misplaced my others."

Mrs. Stanway looked at Joe, and then at the key in his hand. "You haven't locked him inside my office, have you?"

"Um . . ."

"Tell her!" barked Frankie. "Tell her the man's a thief!"

"Well, you see, Mrs. Stanway," said Joe. "That waiter is actually a robber. He's only

working here so he can steal your money!"

"What?" Mrs. Stanway sighed. "Give me the key, please, Joe."

"But, Mrs. Stanway, he really is a thief!"

She took the key from Joe's hand and unlocked the door. The waiter stumbled out, confused and annoyed, with a pair of purple glasses in his hand. "What's going on?"

"Just a misunderstanding, Dale," said Mrs. Stanway. "Thank you for getting my glasses."

The waiter glared at Joe, then stalked off.

"No!" howled Frankie. "He's getting away! Tell her to check the safe, Joe. He's probably got the cash already!"

"Mrs. Stanway, please could you check everything's okay in there?"

"I appreciate your concern, Joe, but really, there's nothing to worry about. Dale's a waiter, not a thief. Look, I'll show you."

She swept inside her office. "See! Nothing's

out of place. And the dial on the safe hasn't moved since I last touched it. Now, I think maybe you'd better get back to the dining room."

"What do we do now?" asked Joe.

Joe and Frankie were in the bathroom, where no one could hear Joe's voice.

"You spy on them in the dining room," said Frankie, "while I keep watch in the hall."

Joe frowned. "What if they've changed their minds? Maybe they've decided not to rob the place after all."

Frankie looked at Joe as if he was stupid. "Then I wouldn't still be here, would I? If my problem was solved, I'd have passed over."

Frankie was right. But Joe was pretty sure the robbers would be extra careful next time to make sure no one saw them sneaking back into the office.

"There you are, Joe." Gran was waiting in the corridor when Joe came out of the bathroom. "The DJ has started playing! Would you like to dance?"

"No!" yelped Frankie. "You've got to watch the waiters!"

"Um, I don't really like dancing . . ."

"Don't be shy, Joe!" Gran linked arms with him and led him through the double doors into the ballroom.

"I like this song!" Gran said as she dragged Joe onto the dance floor. Unfortunately they were the only ones dancing—apart from a group of toddlers.

"Love your moves!" hissed Damian as Joe danced by his cousin.

Joe spun around and blinked as Damian snapped a photo of him. "Ha! Great picture!"

Joe gave him a death stare. Then he spotted Aunt Marion waving to them from a table nearby. "Look, Gran! It's Aunt Marion. I think she wants you to go over to the table. I'll be back in a second."

Joe raced away before Gran could stop him. He dived out of the ballroom and ran straight into Sarah. The glass she was carrying went flying . . .

CRASH!

A puddle of pineapple juice began to spread around her satin shoes.

"JOE! You did that on purpose!"

"I'm sorry . . . It was an accident!"

Everyone was staring. But Joe didn't care. He'd just seen one of the waiters heading out of the room, glancing furtively over his shoulder.

"Got to go!" said Joe.

"Wait! What about this mess?"

CHAPTER TEN

Joe didn't get far. Sarah grabbed his arm and refused to let go until he had mopped up the juice. As soon as they'd finished, Mom appeared.

"Bedtime," she said.

"What? But, Mom!"

She held up her hand. "No, Joe, it's been a long day for everyone . . . Now go and say good night to Gran and Aunt Kate!"

Joe sighed. He knew it was useless to argue. He said good night, then followed Mom and Toby out of the lounge. They passed Uncle Len talking to Mrs. Stanway about the clock in the dining room.

"It's an exceptional piece," Len was saying. "It's probably worth quite a bit."

"How fabulous!" Mrs. Stanway beamed.

Then Frankie spotted Joe and jumped up from his post in the hall. "Where are you going? You can't go to bed now!"

Joe hung back behind Mom and Toby. "Don't worry," he whispered to Frankie. "I'll sneak back down in five minutes."

"Don't be long," wailed Frankie. "There's not much time left—they're bound to strike soon!"

Joe hadn't realized quite how tired he was. As soon as his head hit the pillow, he felt a wave of drowsiness wash over him. *Just a five-minute snooze while Toby drifts off,* he told himself. *Then I'll sneak back downstairs . . .*

"JOE! JOE! WAKE UP!" Frankie was on his bed, licking his face. "You've been gone for ages! It's almost midnight. Everyone's in the ballroom, and the bad waiters are sneaking around. Come on!"

Joe stumbled out of bed and pulled on his shoes.

They crept downstairs into the deserted lobby and sneaked to their hiding place behind the potted plant . . .

After ten minutes or so, they heard footsteps and singing, but it was only Marion and Bob going upstairs to bed.

Joe sighed. The hallway was cold, and he was fed up with Frankie, who was constantly scratching at his stitches. But suddenly

Frankie stopped scratching. "That's weird," Frankie whispered.

"What?"

"The clock in the dining room!" said Frankie. "Look—that wall clock over there says it's five past twelve. But I didn't hear Sylvia's clock in the dining room chime!"

Joe was about to shrug when suddenly he froze. The clock! THE CLOCK! *Of course!* "Frankie," he gasped. "It's not the money they're after. It's the clock!"

Frankie looked at him blankly.

"I heard Uncle Len say it was very valuable," explained Joe. "That's what they're going to steal—Mrs. Stanway's special clock in the dining room! Quick, we're in the wrong place. We've got to stop them!"

They dashed across the hallway. The dining-room lights were off, but Joe could just make out two shadowy figures standing by the mantelpiece. One of them was carrying a large gym bag . . .

"It's them!" Joe shouted.

The men stopped. Then one of them turned and raced toward the kitchen.

The other one—the man carrying the bag— ran toward them, shoving Joe out of the way.

"After him!" barked Frankie.

The thief was already through the door. Frankie raced ahead of him and head-butted an umbrella stand, knocking it straight into the robber's path. But the man just stepped over it—and then into the revolving doors . . .

UNDEAD PETS

Joe snatched up an umbrella from the stand and tried to jam the doors with it. For a moment it worked. But then the thief rattled the door angrily, and the umbrella snapped in two.

"He's getting away!" Joe yelled.

But just then a figure appeared on the other side of the revolving doors. He spotted Joe. He looked at the thief. Then he jammed a battered suitcase in the revolving door.

"Uncle Charlie!" Joe cried.

UNDEAD PETS

The police arrived soon after. They freed Dale the thieving waiter from the revolving doors and immediately arrested him. His accomplice had taken a wrong turn in the kitchen and gotten stuck in the walk-in fridge. The clock was returned undamaged to Mrs. Stanway's mantelpiece in the dining room.

The hotel was buzzing with excitement. Joe and Uncle Charlie were heroes! Mrs. Stanway ordered drinks and snacks for everyone in the lounge, and Joe had to tell and retell his story over and over again.

At last he managed to slip away to the lobby, where Frankie was waiting for him. His tail was wagging and his green eyes were shining. "I'm going now, Joe . . ."

Frankie leaped up and licked Joe's face, smothering him in sticky zombie drool.

By the time Joe had wiped it off, Frankie had gone.

"There you are, Joe!"

He spun around to find Uncle Charlie standing in the shadows watching him.

"Hi, Uncle Charlie. I can't wait to hear about your adventures," said Joe.

Uncle Charlie grinned. "I think maybe I should hear all about your adventures first . . ." He winked at Joe. "They sound much more exciting!"

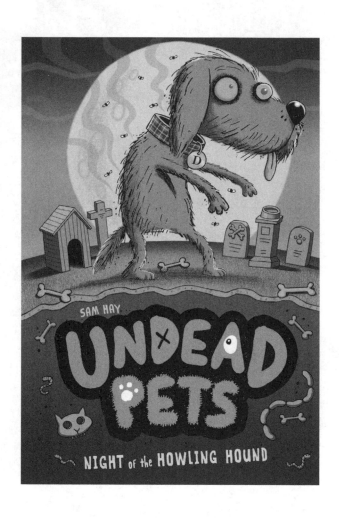

SAM HAY

UNDEAD PETS

NIGHT of the HOWLING HOUND

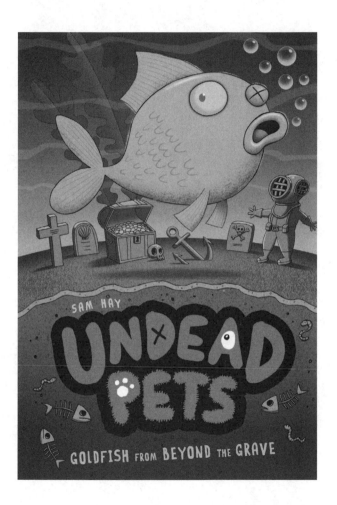

SAM HAY

UNDEAD PETS

GOLDFISH FROM BEYOND THE GRAVE

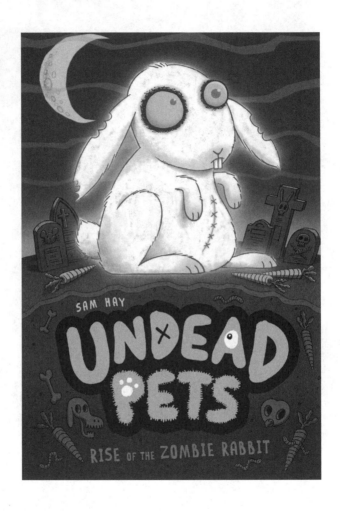

SAM HAY

UNDEAD PETS

FLIGHT OF THE PUMMELED PARAKEET